Standing Tall

Written by Philip Wooderson
Illustrated by Alan Wade

Heinem

D1347849

Chapter 1

Carrie got up early on the day of the spelling test and asked her dad to help her go through the list of words.

'You're good at spelling,' said Dad. 'Don't worry!'

Carrie asked her mum to test her on the way to school. She spelled nearly all the words right, but as they walked up to the school gates, her mum said, 'Last one: **scare**.'

's...c...,' said Carrie, 'a...i...?'

'It's an **r**, not an **i**,' Mum said. 'You got it right with Dad.'

Carrie looked down at the ground. She found learning spellings easy, but this was only the second week at her new school and she still felt nervous. At her old school, she'd had lots of friends, but she didn't have many at her new school yet. She didn't want to go through the school gates.

'Don't worry!' Mum said. 'You'll be all right!'

3

Carrie wasn't so sure. She was quite small for her age and she had a quiet voice, and no one seemed to notice her in class - except Mandy.

Mandy was tall with long, fair hair, and she was clever. She always seemed to get everything right. Everyone wanted to be her friend.

Their teacher was called Miss Wallace. She came in smiling brightly and spent the first few minutes talking about her new pet kitten, called Lola.

'Lola gets very hungry but I'm too busy to go shopping every day. I'm going to buy tins of Meow in packs of three from now on. Here's a sum to work out,' said Miss Wallace. 'If I buy two packs of three tins, how many tins will I have?'

A few children put up their hands, but Miss Wallace looked at Carrie.

Carrie was good at sums. She tried to work this one out, but everybody was looking at her. That made it harder to think. She knew there were twos and threes in the problem.

'Five?' she whispered.

Carrie heard a few children laughing.

'Please be quiet!' said Miss Wallace. 'Do you know the answer, Mandy?'

Mandy grinned at Carrie. 'Six, of course! It's easy-peasy!'

'Good!' said Miss Wallace.

After playtime, it was time for the spelling test. Miss Wallace had written four sets of letters on the board: **air**, **are**, **ere** and **ear**.

'I'll say a sentence, then I'll choose one of you to come and write the word on the board,' said Miss Wallace. 'Let's start with this one: I went to the **fair**.'

A girl called Sandra got it right.

'I saw a big brown **bear**,' said Miss Wallace. Ahmed got that right.

'I want to go over **there**.' Miss Wallace always left the hard ones until last. Mandy spelled **there**.

Miss Wallace said, 'Very good, Mandy! Now, Carrie, you've not put your hand up. Try this one: You can't **scare** me!'

Carrie walked, slowly, up to the board.

'So, Carrie, how do you spell **scare**?' asked Miss Wallace.

Some of the children giggled.
Miss Wallace looked crossly at them.

Carrie began to write on the
board, s... c... a... Then she stopped.
She couldn't remember what came
next. Miss Wallace smiled at Carrie,
and asked, 'What's the next letter?'

'i...?' said Carrie, quietly.

'No, try again,' said Miss Wallace.

'She got it wrong!' Mandy
shouted. 'She put an **i** in, Miss!'

9

'Mandy!' called Miss Wallace. 'Please don't shout out. Carrie, would you like to have another go?'

Carrie wrote **scare** on the board. She got it right this time.

'Well done, Carrie. Good girl,' said Miss Wallace.

Carrie turned and smiled at the rest of the class, but it was nearly playtime and no one really noticed.

After lunch, Carrie went out into the playground. The girls were playing chase.

'Do you want to play?' Sandra called.

'No way!' shouted Mandy. 'She's such a wimp, she'd be no good on our team. We might **scare** her!'

'Don't be mean, Mandy. We all make mistakes,' Sandra said.

'Not all the time!' said Mandy. 'Hey, Carrie - how do you spell **scare**?'

Everyone stared so hard at Carrie that she had to turn away, and she didn't open her mouth again for the rest of the afternoon.

Chapter 2

When Carrie got home, she felt so unhappy, she just sat in front of the television.

She could do sums and spellings just like everyone else. She might even be good at chase if they would just give her a chance.

Carrie could feel something down the side of the chair. She pulled it out. It was one of Mum's magazines. On the cover was a picture of a tall woman.

Carrie looked closely at
the cover.

Keep fit

STANDING TALL!

Do people
make fun
of you?
You need to
stand tall!
Exercises to
stretch you.
Read HOW!

Carrie opened the magazine and read the heading.

STAND TALL, FEEL GOOD, LOOK GOOD!
You've all heard of exercising...
Now try STRETCHY-CISING!

There was a full-page picture of the woman from the cover standing in front of a mirror with her eyes closed. She was smiling.

Carrie started to read the next page. It said:

Take a very deep breath. Pretend an elastic band is fixed to the top of your head. It is pulling your head gently upwards.

This sounded like being tortured, but Carrie read some more:

You feel your back start to stretch. Your neck starts to feel much longer and your head feels as light as a balloon. It starts floating. It rises up into the air until it bumps into the ceiling!

Carrie read this again, then she looked at the picture again, and looked at the title again too.

STAND TALL, FEEL GOOD, LOOK GOOD!
STRETCHY-CISING is easy!

Perhaps it was worth a try. If it worked, it might solve all her problems. So Carrie took the magazine upstairs and went into her parents' bedroom. There was a mirror hanging on the wall. When Carrie looked in the mirror, she could just see the top of her head.

She closed her eyes, took a deep breath, and imagined the elastic band pulling the top of her head. She imagined herself getting taller and taller. She imagined her head feeling so light it started to float slowly up, towards the bedroom ceiling.

Time passed, but her head hadn't touched the ceiling.

At last, Carrie opened her eyes and looked in the mirror again. Now she could see her eyebrows, and her eyes, and her nose, so surely she was a bit taller? Stretchy-cising WAS easy!

If she did it three times a day, she might end up taller than Mandy!

Carrie was so excited, she rushed downstairs to tell Dad, but he was on the phone. When he put the phone down, he said, 'What's made you look so cheerful?'

'It's a secret,' said Carrie. She decided not to tell Dad about stretchy-cising, not yet. She wanted him to notice that she was taller.

'By the way, how did the spelling test go?' asked Dad.

'That's a secret too!' said Carrie, laughing.

Now she was standing taller, she knew she'd feel good and look good!

When she woke up in the morning, she looked in the mirror again. She could still see her eyes and her nose, but only by standing on tiptoe. She needed more stretchy-cising.

'Breakfast!' Mum called from downstairs.

Carrie closed her eyes. She took a deep breath and tried very hard to imagine her back getting straighter and longer. She imagined herself getting taller and taller, and then she imagined her head floating up like a balloon, towards the bedroom ceiling.

She waited. She tried extra hard. And then she opened her eyes to see her mum, staring at her with a puzzled look on her face.

'What are you up to?' asked Mum.

Carrie didn't know what to say.

'Do you think I look taller?' asked Carrie.

Mum smiled. 'Well, maybe just a little bit,' she said. 'But you don't need to worry about that. It's not what you look like that matters, it's what you're like inside.'

Chapter 3

Carrie walked into the classroom, still hoping she looked a bit taller. But nobody seemed to notice because there was a new boy, sitting by himself, looking nervous. Carrie thought he looked almost too small to be in their class.

'This is Sam,' said Miss Wallace. 'I hope you'll all make him feel welcome and help him to make new friends.' Then she asked everyone in the class to tell Sam their name and something about themselves. When it was her turn, Miss Wallace told Sam how naughty her kitten had been. Everyone laughed.

As a special treat to welcome Sam to the class, Miss Wallace asked him to choose a story from one of the big books in the book corner. Sam chose a story about some owls.

Miss Wallace read the story with the class. Afterwards, she asked some questions and everyone put up their hands, except Sam.

Mandy whispered, 'He's so small, you can hardly see him!'

Some of the class started to giggle, and Carrie giggled as well, until she remembered how she'd felt, only the day before. She knew what it was like when everyone was laughing at you, and she felt sorry for Sam.

'Five minutes to playtime,' Miss Wallace said. 'Let's see if we can remember our spellings from yesterday, shall we? How about **scare**?'

That was easy. They all put up their hands.

Carrie shouted, 'Can I write it, Miss?'

'Please don't shout out, Carrie,' said Miss Wallace. 'I wonder if Sam can write it?'

Everyone stared at Sam. His cheeks went as red as tomatoes. Carrie could hear him saying to himself, **s...c...a...r...e**, but he didn't sound very sure about it.

'I'm no good at spelling,' he whispered to Carrie.

'But you know how to spell it!' said Carrie. 'Go and write it on the board!'

Sam walked slowly to the front of the class. He looked small and scared. He started to write, saying each letter as he wrote it:

'**s...c...a...i...**'

'Ha ha!' cried Mandy. 'He's put an **i** in, Miss, just like Carrie did yesterday!' The whole class burst into giggles.

'Mandy! I won't have you calling out in class like that!' called Miss Wallace. She turned to Sam and smiled. 'That was nearly right, Sam. It was very brave of you to give it a try, as you are new to the class. Well done.'

Mandy looked cross because she
had been told off.

As everyone got ready for
playtime, Miss Wallace said to
Carrie, 'You know what it's like to
be new in the class. Will you look
after Sam at playtime?'

Carrie looked for Sam in the
playground, but all she could see
was a crowd of children playing,
shouting and laughing. Carrie
wished she was tall enough to see
what was going on.

She thought about stretchy-cising. She even closed her eyes. But then she heard Mandy shouting, 'You can't play with us, Sam! You can't get anything right!'

Carrie suddenly felt very angry. She stood up straight and called out, 'You don't know everything Mandy! I bet you can't spell **stretchy-cising**!'

Everyone went quiet. Then
Mandy said, 'That's not fair. That's
not a real word!'

'It's not fair to tease people
either,' Carrie said, loud and clear.
'And why should you always
choose who plays chase? I'll play
with you, Sam.'

'So will I,' said Ahmed.

'So will I,' said Frankie.

'Me too,' said Sandra.

Carrie looked at Sam. He was smiling at her, but Carrie thought how small and scared he still looked. As the others ran off to start the game, she walked over to him.

'Are you sure you're okay?' she asked him, kindly. 'Some of the boys run really fast when we're playing chase.'

'I can run fast too,' said Sam, quietly, then he raced off.

Carrie watched him. She had never seen anyone run so fast. He was the best player of chase she had ever seen. Everyone was amazed, as he darted and dashed round the playground.

Carrie could see that Sam felt good. And he looked good too. Sam didn't need stretchy-cising, and nor did Carrie. They were both standing tall now!